The Little PEACOCK

by Mingmei Yip and Pimlada Phuapradit

W
FRANKLIN WATTS
LONDON•SYDNEY

For many years, the Peacock Fairy
had helped lots of people.
But now she was getting old. Her feathers
were starting to turn white.

I must teach the secret of my magic to an apprentice, she thought.

The Peacock Fairy put up posters
all around the town announcing
a competition at the palace.
All the young peacocks were very excited.

Little peacock stopped to read a poster.
"It would be amazing to be an apprentice,"
he thought.

Soon, the Peacock Fairy's palace was full of peacocks. Their beautiful tails looked like painted Chinese fans.

"You all look beautiful," said the Peacock Fairy, "but you all look the same. I need one of you to be different from the rest. Come back tonight in time for the firework festival. Before the festival starts I will pick my new apprentice."

Little Peacock walked home.

"I would like to be the apprentice,"

he thought to himself. "But how can I

make myself look different?"

After a while, he passed an old woman.

She looked sad.

"What's the matter?" asked Little Peacock.

"No one will buy my peaches,"

said the old woman.

Little Peacock pulled out a handful
of his colourful feathers and gave them
to the old woman.

"You can sell these," he said.

Soon the feathers were all sold.

"Thank you," said the old woman, smiling.

Along the road, Little Peacock met

an old man, working in the fields.

He waved his arms in the air.

"What's wrong?" asked Little Peacock.

"I am too hot," the old man gasped.

Little Peacock plucked some
feathers for the old man.
"Please take these to fan yourself."
And the man did.

Next, the little peacock saw a mother
holding a baby.

The baby wouldn't stop crying.

"Please can you spare some money so I can
buy some warm clothes for my baby?"
asked the mother.

"I don't have any money, but here are some feathers to keep your baby warm," said Little Peacock.

Covered with feathers, the baby stopped crying and smiled.

It was getting late. Little Peacock
was nearly home. As he passed a hut,
he heard a mother say,
"Son, you must stay in bed to get well!"
"But Mother, if I can go to
the firework festival and see
the fireworks, I know I will get better."

Little Peacock had forgotten all about`
the fireworks. Now he had given
away all his feathers, he would not be able
to show off his colourful tail at the festival.
Little Peacock felt sad.

At midnight, all the peacocks gathered in the Peacock Fairy's palace. They all looked their best, but Little Peacock looked like a chicken with no feathers!

"What has happened to all your feathers?" she asked Little Peacock.

"I gave them to people who needed them more than me," the Little Peacock replied.

The Peacock Fairy smiled.

"You have a kind heart," she said. "And now you look different from the rest. You shall be my apprentice."

Then the Peacock Fairy used her magic.
In a flash, Little Peacock had a tail full of
the most beautiful colourful feathers you
have ever seen.

When he flew up to the sky his feathers
looked just like a sparkling fireworks display!
In time, he too became a wise and helpful
Peacock Fairy.

Story order

Look at these 5 pictures and captions.
Put the pictures in the right order
to retell the story.

1

Little Peacock has no feathers left!

2

The Peacock Fairy chooses her apprentice.

3

Little Peacock helps an old man.

4

Little Peacock has the most amazing tail!

5

Little Peacock sees the Peacock Fairy's poster.

Independent Reading

This series is designed to provide an opportunity for your child to read on their own. These notes are written for you to help your child choose a book and to read it independently.

In school, your child's teacher will often be using reading books which have been banded to support the process of learning to read. Use the book band colour your child is reading in school to help you make a good choice. *The Little Peacock* is a good choice for children reading at Purple Band in their classroom to read independently.

The aim of independent reading is to read this book with ease, so that your child enjoys the story and relates it to their own experiences.

About the book

In this traditional Chinese tale, Little Peacock aims to become Peacock Fairy's new apprentice. But how can he make himself stand out? By helping others, he gives away all his feathers. But this lesson in kindness is exactly what the Peacock Fairy was looking for. So Little Peacock becomes a worthy apprentice, after all.

Before reading

Help your child to learn how to make good choices by asking: "Why did you choose this book? Why do you think you will enjoy it?" Look at the cover together and ask: "What do you think the story will be about?" Ask your child to think of what they already know about the story context. Then ask your child to read the title aloud. Ask: "How would you describe the two peacocks on the cover. What are the differences?" Remind your child that they can sound out the letters to make a word if they get stuck.

Decide together whether your child will read the story independently or read it aloud to you.

During reading

Remind your child of what they know and what they can do independently. If reading aloud, support your child if they hesitate or ask for help by telling the word. If reading to themselves, remind your child that they can come and ask for your help if stuck.

After reading

Support comprehension by asking your child to tell you about the story. Use the story order puzzle to encourage your child to retell the story in the right sequence, in their own words. The correct sequence can be found on the next page.

Give your child a chance to respond to the story: "How do you think Little Peacock felt when he entered the Peacock Fairy's palace for the first time? How would you feel?"

Help your child think about the messages in the book that go beyond the story and ask: "Why do you think the Peacock Fairy chose to reward Little Peacock? What do you think Little Peacock learned by helping others?"

Extending learning

Help your child predict other possible outcomes of the story by asking: "What do you think would happen if Little Peacock decided to keep all his feathers?"

In the classroom, your child's teacher may be teaching how to use speech marks when characters are speaking. There are many examples in this book that you could look at with your child. Find these together and point out how the end punctuation (comma, full stop, question mark or exclamation mark) comes inside the speech marks. Ask the child to read some examples out loud, adding appropriate expression.

Franklin Watts
First published in Great Britain in 2021
by The Watts Publishing Group

Series Editors: Jackie Hamley and Melanie Palmer
Series Advisors and Development Editors: Dr Sue Bodman and Glen Franklin
Series Designers: Peter Scoulding and Cathryn Gilbert

A CIP catalogue record for this book is
available from the British Library.

ISBN 978 1 4451 7420 4 (hbk)
ISBN 978 1 4451 7421 1 (pbk)
ISBN 978 1 4451 8241 4 (ebook)
ISBN 978 1 4451 7476 1 (library ebook)

Printed in China

Franklin Watts
An imprint of
Hachette Children's Group
Part of The Watts Publishing Group
Carmelite House
50 Victoria Embankment
London EC4Y 0DZ

An Hachette UK Company
www.hachette.co.uk

www.franklinwatts.co.uk

Answer to Story order: 5,3,1,2,4